# Fractals:
## Short Stories

# Fractals:
## Short Stories

Joanna Walsh

First published in 2013
By 3:AM Press, an imprint of Murdo Ltd.
3ampress.co.uk

© Joanna Walsh 2013

The right of the authors to be identified as the Authors of the Work has been asserted by them in accordance with the Copyright, Designs and Patents Act 1988. All rights reserved. No part of this publication may be reproduced, stored in a retrieval system, or transmitted, in any form or by any means without the prior written permission of the publisher, nor be otherwise circulated in any for of binding or cover other than that in which it is published without a similar condition being imposed on the subsequent purchaser.

Cover design by Chrystal Ding
Typeset by Susan Tomaselli

First Edition
ISBN 978-0-9926842-0-4

## CONTENTS

| | |
|---|---:|
| And After... | 3 |
| Femme Maison | 7 |
| Shhh... | 13 |
| Hauptbanhof | 17 |
| Reading Habits | 25 |
| Summer Story | 29 |
| Exes | 35 |
| Half the World Over | 39 |
| Blue | 47 |
| Fin de Collection | 51 |

# And After...

*For Emily Dickinson*

LET IT BE AUTUMN.

Let it be another town. Let the houses be lowrise, undistinguished, a mix of old and new. Let the doctor's surgery in a terraced sidestreet be new sandbrick with a porthole window and double doors, and thick brightly-coloured metal bars at waist height to steady the entering infirm.

Let the branches of chain stores in the high street be too small to carry the full range. Let their sales be undermined by charity shops selling just as good as new. Let there be other shops stocking nothing useful: handicrafts; overpriced children's clothes; holidays on window cards, faded; homemade homewares. Let these shops be unvisited and kept by old women still peering from doorways expecting their ideal customer. Let fashion be something heard of somewhere else.

Let there be backalleys for cycles hungover with brambles, with cidercans in ditches. Let these backways be quicker ways but let no one question the cars. Let these ways snake along the back of allotments and supermarkets and h-block schools on the ring road. Let the ways snake under the ring road. Let dogwalkers use them: let anglers use them, and junkies. Let these ways be deserted when the children are in school, except for the odd dogwalker or angler or junkie. Let each wear his particular uniform. Let no angler or dogwalker be mistaken for a junkie: let no junkie be mistaken for a dogwalker or angler. Let anglers only occasionally walk dogs.

Let there be children and old people but few whose occupation is neither hope nor memory. Let there have been immigration at some point: enough to fill the convenience stores, the foreign restaurants, but let it be forgotten. Let the children be all in school, a breath held in, released at 3 o'clock across the park. Let the town's rhythm be unquestioned. Let me be single: no children, no family. Let me not fit in.

Let there be a college where art students dream of cities they do not leave for.

Let art for the old people be something colourful and, for the young people, something black. Let their art be always things. Let the colourful things appear sometimes in the windows of the shops that sell homemade homewares. Let the art students sometimes fill an empty shop lot with black things. Let the old people go right up to the windows of the empty shop lot and squint and frown.

Let there be a coffee shop next to a head shop where the art students hang out, and where I buy a gypsy scarf with tassels. Let my purchase mean I am considered arty.

Let the coffee shop serve bad coffee. Let it have only yesterday's news and the local papers (let small crimes occur, and let occasional larger crimes, on the outskirts of town beyond the ring road, be personally motivated, down to nothing more than bad marriages, bad upbringings). Let me sit in the coffee shop and, while drinking bad coffee, hear the rumour that someone famous was to come to town but that the visit was cancelled. Let the woman behind the counter shake her head, her towelled hand continuing to spiral in the persistently streaked glass.

# Femme Maison

YOU WANTED TO LOOK DIFFERENT FOR HIM. YOU WANTED A CHANGE of a dress. You wanted a new dress you had never seen before. You wanted to be someone else, someone neither of you knew.

But then you have not met Him yet.

He will take you away from all this. As things are, you can't go on in any way: everything is missing. If you were somewhere else, you would already be wearing the different dress, a summer dress. You would be comfortable. But the dress you have is too big. You can't wear your dress if you can't alter it, and you don't have sewing machine needles. You broke the last one and the shop didn't have any more.

You were typing on your laptop: something important, you can't remember, but you began to search for sewing machine needles.

It's the same all over the house. You go to look for things but they are always in the wrong room. Where are they? They might have been left outside in the rain. They might have been put on a high shelf so the children would not get them.

No sooner is there something to do than it requires something else to do it with. The piece of information needed is always at one remove: scribbled on an envelope already in the recycling; printed on an old bank statement, perhaps shredded; written in a letter filed in the cabinet you don't open any more.

It's question of systems. Go upstairs and you'll notice a tea towel that should be in the kitchen. Bring it down and there are the books that should be by your bed. How did they change places? Why didn't you notice the books before you went upstairs for the tea towel? Then you could have taken them up and put them by the bed and picked up the tea towel and taken it down. Except it wasn't the tea towel you went to look for, was it? It was something else, but exactly what you can't remember.

Sewing machine needles.

You should have established some kind of process.

There *is* a process to the day. You eat at established times though it's such a bother to make. Always afterwards you find a wrapper without a name snaking across the kitchen surface. What is is from? If it is vacant, why was it not cleared? How did you miss it? On tables small things migrate according to the season: the seals from plastic milk cartons, beer bottle lids (though is was He who drank beer whereas you drink wine). How did they get there? Why were they not removed? There must be a way to get rid of them.

You forget to wash your hands before re-opening your laptop. Its keys are slick with butter. At least not with jam but this is because the jam is still in the shop where you forgot to buy it. You came away with 250g of cherries and a pint of milk. The milk you needed, undoubtedly. You needed cocoa but they did not have cocoa. The queue was long and you were distracted by the labels of the wine bottles behind the counter, not the bottles with graphics and fancy typography but the bottles with pictures of chateaux, sea bays, farmhouses. You walked into each of these landscapes, as if you were visiting. If you were in those places, any of those places, you could wear the dress instead of tight urban jeans, the dress that needs altering. You could have been comfortable.

You go into the post office in case there is something else you need. Each time you go in you look at the magazines and consider buying *Vogue*. You do not buy it. Next time you shop you will do the same thing.

All your life you've been asked to choose: to be the woman who didn't drink canned sodas, who didn't watch American television programmes, who would never, even in fun, decorate her home with Anaglypta wallpaper. Some of these injunctions you have overturned, but there are always fresh ones. You choose not to choose any more.

It's not only your fault. After the children left, bit by bit you and He abandoned the house, eating takeaways, spending evenings in cafes. At one point you had been able to afford to eat out every weekend. But the house missed you. The fresh flowers you bought were, it knew, an insult, a sop. That's why you knew He had to go.

## FEMME MAISON

But how did your keyboard get so dirty? The dust builds all over the house, always on a different surface. You chase it with a corner of the dress's sleeve. The dirt is still there, grey and furry. It has merely transferred. You are now part of it.

After He was gone, things altered. You expanded into the areas of the house you hadn't previously used: the study, the front room. You felt, for the first time, that they were yours. You also felt you owed it to them.

But the house is still not a perfect fit. Still things surprise you. When you try to get to the cupboard holding the dusters, there is something in the way: a stand of washing, a tall stool from the counter. Who put them there?

You turn, you remember—the laptop. You had forgotten. You remember. You had got up. You had wanted to clean the keyboard. You had gone to find a duster.

Something was altered. What was it?

Wait. You remember.

You had cut but you had not pasted.

Your words hover in vacant space. You turn. You run. You will save them.

You paste. They are still there.

How could you have left them? How could you have forgotten? How did you manage to leave your thought at its waist to search for the duster? How did you fail to get the duster but return to the laptop?

What you had written might have been lost forever. The words are still there. But so is the dust.

You thought it would be OK after He was gone. You thought you'd have more time for work, for fusslessness. But the house is relentless.

The fridge must occasionally be defrosted. Something knocks in the icebox. Frost has grown on the walls of the cool section as moss does on a tomb but inverse, its fingers reaching down towards the salad drawer. An afternoon hacking though the ice forest may reach a single embryonically suspended fish finger.

You still attempt to generate one bag of rubbish each week: the bin demands it. The dishwasher is completely redundant. The washing machine begs to be used but your piles of laundry are dwindling, pathetic. They barely skim the bottom of the drum: they are hardly dirty.

Vines slap agains the window. On the patio the barbecue is rotting, the lawnmower is rusting. How are you meant to attack the overgrowing jasmine? With the blunted shears? With the kitchen scissors?

Some things used to matter so much: the exact shade of green of the garden chairs, which did not match the exact shade of green of the garden table. Now both are sun-bleached, flaking. 'A Generous Family House.' That's what the estate agent said when he came to value it, 'Generous.' For a few weeks he sent you emails: would you sell? But that was years ago.

The machines wait patiently. They must wait. In the daily round, certain chairs must be sat in.

You put the dress into the washing machine. It will be clean before it is altered. You add detergent, switch it on. The drum goes round and round. The dress is not dirty but perhaps dusty. The dust travels from the dress to the inside of the washing machine, then out through the tubes. The house senses an exchange. It is satisfied.

Shhh…

THE WOMEN CHERISH THEIR ILLNESSES / JEALOUSLY. THE OTHER women / disapprove.

One, / when she had cancer, stayed / at a hotel beside a stream. One / of the other women said that she would rather be at home, without / the fuss, despite / the mess, in the bo- / som of her family.

One / has allergies / meaning she cannot eat / what other women give her. In restaurants she is visible, sends / things back, demands / do you have..? asks / can you make..? says / I don't want it like... The other women can hear her / across the room. They whisper. I am not immune. /

My mother-in-law, misguidedly, / after an episode of joint inflammation, decided / to eat only meat and fat (with some green vegetables). As I am / a pauper she was difficult to care for: eggs / for breakfast instead of cheap / cereal, toast, / spreads: / steak / for lunch (my husband insisted) and always the refusal, righteous, / safe / of bread. I tried / to underfeed her. I served / her with a scowl, with scepticism (her regime, her own creation): I said / nothing.

The men / do not have these types / of illnesses or, if they do,/ they don't have these effects. The men / do not / notice the womens' illnesses. Or if they do, they do not say so. / Shhh.

At the hotel beside the stream there was no / noise / except/ the stream swishing. It soothed her,/ the cancer woman. Perhaps / there were also rushes. Exceptionally, / there was room service, silver cutlery, un- / stained towels.

## JOANNA WALSH

The women envy each other's illnesses / scheme to concoct new ones. / However true, however frail they feel, part of them knows / their pain will piss off / the other women.

# Hauptbahnhof

*"TWO-WAY PROPOSITIONS: IN THE FIRST EXAMPLE, THE PREPOSITIONAL phrase describes a destination. In the second, it describes a location. German indicates this distinction through the use of cases (Wohin/where to? Wo/Where at?)."*

I know what you are thinking.

But it is possible to sleep on the station.

If you don't look like a tramp, if you change your clothes with reasonable regularity, above all if you look like you are waiting for someone.

I have perfected the waiting look.

After all, even if I am no longer sure whether I am waiting, or whether I only wish to appear to be waiting, it is my responsibility not to cause a 'situation', an incident. It is my responsibility to protect the people who pass through the station from the sight of a woman alone who is not waiting for anyone. Although, of course, I am.

And there is no better place to wait than the Hauptbahnhof. It is large enough for me to change platforms regularly. It is clean.

There are vastly fewer pigeons than in any other grand central station in Europe.

The Hauptbahnhof smells of coffee, of floor polish, of cigarettes, of the substances we use to correct, to mark time, to keep ourselves together. Of course smoking is banned but this is difficult to police. Before they board their train, people will always want a last cigarette.

I pride myself on travelling light. Waiting, it is necessary to look as if you are expecting an arrival, or as if you are about to depart: conversely you must change platforms with reasonable regularity if you are to avoid the attention of the authorities. For both of these purposes, a small, light suitcase is ideal.

The Hauptbahnhof is open 24/7. Coincidences arrive at any time of day or night.

## JOANNA WALSH

I have become used to the sound of trains. There are two noises: the solid hum of the wheels on the track, and the lighter rattle of the upper parts of the rolling stock. Sometimes it seems laughable that they coincide.

Naturally I was disappointed you did not meet me. When I arrived I searched for you on the platform, thinking you had missed me in the crowd, had got the wrong Level. After a while I realised this was unlikely: the Signs mean that it is impossible to miss a train. If you know how to read the Signs, that is.

That night, I had trouble with the Signs. When I didn't see you I decided you must be waiting at your apartment. Perhaps there had been a confusion, or an engagement you had failed to mention. You had not sent your address but, knowing the name of your U-bahn stop, I went to the stationer's on Level 0. At the stand with tourist books I dismissed the maps showing Berlin page by page. I needed to know where you were and where I was at the same time. I needed to see the whole city.

    I slipped a map from its plastic compartment at the back of a city guide. Berlin was bigger than I expected. The map unfolded and unfolded until, under its own weight, it collapsed against itself, a long tear snaking across its centre.

The sound was deafening.

I had intended to steal the map having, surely, more need of it than anyone else. But the noise embarrassed me so much that I quickly refolded and stuffed it back into its plastic envelope.

I walked from the station a short distance across Europaplatz to steps leading down into the mouth of what looked like the underground. At the end of a white tunnel, I came upon two platforms, both empty, their Signs describing stops I did not recognise from the U-Bahn map. I took an up escalator, hoping for further platforms, but found myself back under the crystal dome of the station.

It was only later that I discovered the U-bahn is not yet connected to the Hauptbahnhof.

Of course I did not then speak German.

But I have improved (you would be proud).

# HAUPTBANHOF

The level 1 branch of Relay contains magazines from fifteen different countries. There are also phrase books, dictionaries and newspapers. It is possible, with time on your hands, to learn a language.

That first night I called you a couple of times but you didn't answer. It's possible I got your number wrong. I emailed you regarding this but you did not reply. I thought perhaps you were playing games, that you would relent or that, when we met, you would provide some good reason. Maybe it was a joke. I thought your phone was out of charge, that you had no connection. I thought you had lost it, that it had been stolen. I thought you were busy, were unavoidably detained, would answer later. I thought you had been arrested or were in hospital. I thought you were dead. There were so many possible explanations: I saw no reason not to hope.

In the meantime my diet is not what I might have wished but it is not expensive. As portions are large, it is possible to buy food only once each 24 hours and there is variety. I have become familiar with international cuisine and each day I choose my destination. Dunkin' Donuts has the cheapest coffee, Starbucks the most expensive. They are virtually next door to each other, separated only by the hairdresser. This is not the sort of hairdresser I would normally visit—the type of place with posters of women whose hair is bleached and artificially stiff—but it is necessary to keep up appearances as we may meet at any time. With care, a blow-dry lasts all week, after which there is dry shampoo.

You might think have I regretted my light packing and tired of my single lipstick but the station's selection of cosmetic outlets and chemists means I can try a new shade every day. Sometimes a demonstrator makes me over to look like someone new. For the same reason, my skin has never looked better. I hear that changing your regime regularly renders products more effective (I have become up-to-date with the latest skincare developments).

Sometime deodorising can be a problem but, if you don't mind using the spray kind with CFCs, you can generally get a squirt while the assistant is looking the other way.

Do I miss home? How would I? On the highest Level there is a shop with things for houses. Lifelike plastic dummies sit in deckchairs in the window. Everything is new, perfect. Things are bought and taken away and replaced by new new things. Nothing in the Hauptbahnhof ever wears out.

You would have thought the shopgirls might recognise me after all this time, but they never do, only at the hairdressers where my details are on file so I get my regular stylist.

So many people pass through here…

The one difficulty is recharging my phone. I'm telling you this so you know why I cannot always be in touch. Not wanting to draw attention to my waiting, I am reluctant to ask in shops or at the ticket office, and am only occasionally able to clandestinely use the socket in Relay which, I presume, is for powering the vacuum cleaner.

How do I continue to support myself? Yes I know what you are thinking—but no need for that. I am not penniless. I do not have to pay for accommodation. My funds are not infinite. However I am economical, and I do not expect to wait forever.

I resent that I have to pay for water.

Using the dictionaries, the newspapers, the phrase books, I have arrived in my studies at German prepositions of time and place: nach (to/after/towards/by and still), and jetzt (up to/now/not yet and only just).

It is only sometimes that I think you are, perhaps, not still living in Berlin.

I heard you were in Edinburgh, a city where the station sits in a cleft between two green banks, its rails going merely forwards and back. From the street you look down on lines which braid but do not cross. There are no right angles—no Levels—only one long track into Scotland and another into England.

If you are in Edinburgh, you will have to return. I know you may take a plane but I understand a line will soon connect Hauptbahnhof to the airport. I can wait. Yes, there are buses, but that's not your style. If you have become famous in Scotland, there is always the possibility you may take a taxi, but I think it unlikely.

I prefer Departures to Arrivals, by which time everything has already happened. Even as dawn approaches in long lozenges of broken light, Arrivals do not notice the beautiful station. They look down, headed for something known, for home, for bed. Of course

## HAUPTBANHOF

some are met, but fewer than you would think, and they don't stick around. Heroics are reserved for Departures: brave looks, last embraces, minutes slowed by kisses.

Surely everyone who lives in Berlin must pass through the Hauptbahnhof. It is only a matter of time.

Soon they will build the U-bahn link. In the meantime I will wait at Arrivals. If I read the Signs correctly, as I now can, I will not miss a single one.

It is good to know exactly where you are.

# Reading Habits

H WRITES BOOKS FOR PEOPLE WHO KNOW MORE ABOUT MATHS THAN her, for the few people who know more about linguistics, and for general readers who may expect anything or nothing.

S is clever and well-educated but a bad reader. SL is a good reader but badly educated. G is better educated but a bad reader, and not so clever either.

None of them will read books by H.

W used to read novels but now reads, almost exclusively, biographies and histories. W is married to M, who went through a period a few years ago, around when her children were born, when she read only fashion magazines. Although she is now an accomplished reader tackling Dostoyevsky, Lacan, Foucault, she feels she should not miss issues of the fashion magazines and must read these too.

B's husband, G, dictates what B reads. She likes to read what he buys and does not think of it as dictation, but she never buys a book for herself. Sometimes B chooses books from libraries but, as the books will not continue to live with her, she does not see this as rebellion. G sees himself as an independent reader: he buys all the books on the literary prize lists.

P, who is married to SL, reads detective stories, comic fantasy, and books about people who were young at the same time as he was young. These latter are biographies or autobiographies.

When O offers P a book, he feels strangely insulted.

F, who is married to S, reads the same kind of books as S, but not at her instigation.

At the end of each book, because both are intelligent, each is mystified by his or her disappointment. Still they continue to read.

L reads books for work. She is a writer. She enjoys reading them, but they are for work too. L is careful with her reading diet and feels bloated by books she does not like, or which do not contribute to her work. L reads books in one language. M reads books in two languages, N (L's husband) in three. O can read books in four. All the rest read books in one.

The children of H, W and M, L and N, F and S, read batches of similar books designed for children of their respective ages. Next year, they will move onto the next batch.

The children of G and B are grown up. One of them is married to S.

The children of P and SL are grown up. One of them is O.

O reads the same book again and again, sitting in the small bedroom he still occupies in his parents' house.

L, M, N and O would all read books by H. M has read one of H's books; N, two plus an unpublished manuscript which he is reviewing for a literary journal. The others have not actually read any books by H but mean to, except O, who would not. M once asked W to read a book by H but he refused and she felt an surprising sense of personal rejection.

None of the other people mentioned would read books by H.

# Summer Story

IT'S THE DRY POINT OF THE YEAR AND I'VE BEEN WAITING FOR AN answer for some time.

No one's doing anything. There are not enough people left in town to eat all the fruit in the supermarkets. It piles up, 2/3 price, then half price, then finally returns to the back room on tall steel trollies.

The night I slept with you, it rained. You wore a shirt which, although we'd only met a couple of times before, I felt was unusual for you. You wore a jacket with a mend on the elbow that spiralled in concentric circles. But in the morning you looked, not as you had looked the night before, but as you had the other times I'd met you, and you smelled slightly of cigarettes and furniture polish.

In bed you asked whether I wanted to do what I was doing every time I did it. As if you couldn't tell without, as though you'd checked yourself and remembered some rule. And you laughed small and inward each time I said something to you, each time you said something to me. It couldn't possibly have been real. And at the end you said, wow, like someone smacking his lips after a meal. You might have enjoyed it truly but it was an acceptable expression.

The river is at a high point now though the weather is finally hot.

D took me swimming in the river. D is a writer. There are women it is dangerous to talk to. D is one. You try to tell them something, and they start telling you a story about yourself. Before you know it you are pinned, can't move. I wanted to tell D everything, including about you, but I didn't. Feeling the wet air suspended all around me, I closed myself down like windows before a storm. Afterwards I'm glad I did.

...

I heard you were having a party, elsewhere. You—you hardly qualify for the name—had arranged to meet me twice but had cancelled both times. When you sent a message saying you could not meet me, your tense slipped. You said you'd really wanted to see me again. I'd feared it was too true. There'd been a point at which you'd wanted to see me, but it wasn't now. Beware of men who use the past, or the future, too much. I'm twice shy, and you are the third.

You have invited my friend to your party, but not me, the friend of whom I said that I wondered that you didn't like her, not me: she is prettier. And you said, *Oh the British and their blondes.*

You are not British. You are from elsewhere. Your party is for a holiday from elsewhere. I thought you were not the sort to celebrate, but it seems you are. I haven't heard from you for a week, haven't seen you for almost a month now. My blonde friend, who is not British, will ask whether you will see me at the weekend. I will find out what is happening—perhaps. And maybe we will meet next week.

...

You are having another party. This time you have asked me. I am wary. It was a general invite sent out to friends. The email came only an hour ago: there has been an age of strategy since then. How best to reply?

I don't. But I go.

On my way to the party I expose myself to the awful point in London between work and social in which nothing can happen. The libraries have closed, the cafes have closed. The pubs are open, but I don't feel like drinking; the restaurants are open but I don't feel like eating—and I don't want to spend the money. Should I have a cocktail before the party, for courage? Or would I arrive with too much of its evidence on my lips, in my cheeks? Should I walk the streets (if it is not raining)? Could I read, write, in the corner of one of the big cafe-like pubs, inconspicuously enough? Could I shift time from this moment to add elsewhere, to add to other times, times spent—speculatively—with you? With all the time I have, I could learn a language, I could read a book, I could write a book.

In the end I walk nowhere and the wind gets up and the rain starts and it is still too early to go to your party. It is colder than I thought it would be. I didn't know it could be so cold on a warm day.

I get drunk at your party. You don't talk to me. I go into the bedroom and your clothes explode from the wardrobe, violent with dry-cleaning bags. You'll be elsewhere soon. I know you don't mean to stay. Already, you've been gone a while.

...

Oh there were nice times that summer, but they were attached to the wrong people: dashing through the rain with B, with whom I didn't want a relationship, although he did. He took my bracelet and said he could smell my perfume there, a medieval love token. I thought this over-elaborate but the sun shone and the rain at the same time and there were puddles that looked deep and reflected the sunwashed sky.

But that was in July when it rained. Now it's hot enough to stand outside pubs at night and although there are not enough people in town to eat all the fruit in the supermarkets, there are sometimes still parties.

It never hurts to ask (that's what you said to me).
    That's not true.
    Sometimes it hurts to ask.
    The difficulty is working out the right point in time.
    As you still haven't answered my emails I have waited for you in various places hoping you might turn up.

Finally I saw you last night at a party and you ignored me until at last you took me aside and said you were *sort of seeing someone else,* and I said, *s'okay* and you shrugged and said, *that's how it goes,* and I shrugged and said, *that's how it goes.* And when you said it you were quite close to me and you were wearing the jacket you'd worn when we met with the mend at the elbow, and suddenly I felt I could reach out and grab the mend and pull you towards me and kiss you but that wasn't possible any more, though I'd come to the party hoping you would be there and hoping it might have been. And I was wearing the jacket I had on when we met, and when we met it had been draped around my shoulders and every time you kissed me it had fallen off one shoulder and you'd reached your arm around me to pull it back on.

For tonight's party, I'd put a temporary tattoo of a spider on my wrist because I'd thought it would be fun.

Elsewhere in the party L was talking with his work junior, M, and he said, *you're my Dalston homegirl*, and she snarled, *yeah man*, because she wasn't: she was just younger than him and a woman and not white.
    Then L said, *make me a rollie, M*.
    And she rolled one for him, thin and black.

It was not a fun party.

At least I didn't create a fuss, make a scene. At least I didn't leave inelegantly.
    Elegance is a function of failure. The elegant always know what it is to have failed. There is no need for elegance in success: success itself is enough. But elegance in failure is essential.
    I left silently and walked over the bridge on the Thames to the Tube and it was not raining and nobody knew I had gone.

We don't talk now but sometimes I still like to see whether you are on Talk. I can see when you're there because next to your name on my screen there's the little green light. Go, it says, go on, where's the harm in asking?

I have the same green light. It says, available.

# Exes

SOME PEOPLE ARE PROLIFIC WITH XS. SOME USE A SINGLE X, SOME several small xxxs. Some of them put a number of xs before their names, which are sometimes initials, so that there are more xs than anything else. Some of them put the xs after their names, which are longer than the xs: these people are more likely to use a single x. Some of the xs are unexpected, like the single x from someone who flirted with me, but who withdrew his attentions so that the persistent x seemed insincere, impertinent. Some of them are from people who use too many xxxxxs and oblige me to use too many in return. Most are from friends. Few are from lovers, who tend to drop the xs when they are interested, resume them when they are serious, then drop them again when they no longer feel involved. Only one is from a person whose name is X, who I slept with once, and who decided not to see me again, which is confusing as I no longer know whether the X is his initial or a term of endearment.

Half the World Over

# I. Fractals

*A fractal is a mathematical set that has a fractal dimension that usually exceeds its topological dimension and may fall between the integers. Fractals are typically self-similar patterns, where self-similar means they are "the same from near as from far". Fractals may be exactly the same at every scale, or they may be nearly the same at different scales. The definition of fractal goes beyond self-similarity per se to exclude trivial self-similarity and include the idea of a detailed pattern repeating itself.*

YOU LOOK AT YOUR FEET AT THE END OF THE BATH. THEY ARE STILL quite plump and pink. You are waiting for the day blue veins will stick up from them, when a yellow knob will angle the joint of the big toe. That will be when you will have ended up. It will only be for a short time, certainly, but it will be the achievement of life. You have always wanted to be old. The rest, the unwrinkled plumpness, is a fake, a mere waiting.

You have travelled to a literary festival where you are lionised, though no one in this country has read your work. You are put up at an expensive hotel where you are sad to find there is a gym but no swimming pool.

First-off you have a disappointment. You wanted to buy your ex-husband a book signed by the keynote speaker, but it turns out she will not speak until after you will have left.

You spend your days working: panels, seminars, interviews. The people here want to know you. You have little free time.

In your hours of leisure no sooner do you go somewhere than you want to be somewhere else; no sooner are you sitting than you want to be walking; no sooner eating eggs than you want to be eating chocolate.
    Always you wish to be in two places at the same time, always you want to be connected.

Here it does not seem possible.

In this city the streets are straight and cross each other at right angles. It is easy to find your way. The buildings are either very high or very low. The shops say what they are on their fronts, vans go by with signs like Tip Top Butchers, house numbers are prominently displayed.

People tell you to take the tram but the distances they describe do not seem far to you. You walk and you walk.

You shiver in your jacket and thin dress but you do not want to wear the other clothes you brought with you. You go into shops where the clothes do not suit you but, because you are not at home, you do not mind, though you do not buy anything. You walk some more, and all the time you walk you think you should be sitting.

In the cafes you sit then shift chairs to get a better position, a new view. The girls here wear their hair in knots on the tops of their heads. This is just like everywhere else. It seems always to be time for breakfast. A man bends down to feed his chow a strip of bacon. Out of habit you order soup, the cheapest item on the menu. You return to the counter to ask for butter. You are always hungry, always a meal behind.

You cannot communicate with your children, your ex-husband. To be connected you must stand very near a wall of glass.

Outside the cafe a homeless man is shouting *What happened? What was it? Does anybody know? Can anybody explain it to me?* His face is bleeding. He cannot leave the circuit of these streets.

But you like being here. At the hotel, where there is a restaurant at which you cannot afford to eat but where there is also a bowl of free apples in the lobby, the women behind the desk address you in French. On the 37th floor you sleep on your usual side of the bed.

...

You walk out of town to a sea you have never seen before. You intend to reach down and touch it, which you have never done before, so when you return to your own country you can say you have touched it, but in the event it is too cold and smells of seaweed.

## HALF THE WORLD OVER

All around events are advertised for children: they have given up on the adults. They have given up on everything here that is old: age is accelerated in this young country by the sea. Salt rots the ironwork's optimistic balconies.

You intend to enjoy walking along the pier but it is not possible. No one sees that you did not touch the sea. No one sees that you did not enjoy your walk.

...

At the festival's closing party you ask the head of a television network to show you the river. It is midnight and he has stood talking with his arm around you all night, but when you ask about the river, he says he is married.

You mention a friend who has travelled here. When you say friend, say acquaintance, say how do you say ex-nearly-lover? You describe him and what he does without calling him any of this, hoping to see his reflection jump into your listeners' eyes.

A writer gives you a copy of his book, yellowed along the edges. There must be a stack of them at home.

The man in the cafe wipes his chow's mouth with a paper napkin. *What happened? Can anybody explain it to me?*

You become worried that the head of the television network might have thought you wanted him for his power and his money.

From the 37th floor at dusk you can see the lights going on below, snaking the gridded streets. And at dawn someone is swimming in a pool on a lower rooftop. Everything is so like what you would like New York to be like. Perhaps now you will delay going to New York in case it is not enough like this.

Tap, bath, toe. Soon you will be going away. You will not see the writer or the chow or the homeless man or the head of the television network again.

Luckily there are so very many new places in the world.

## II. Notre Dame

Sitting in the cafe opposite, I am happy because I am not one of the tourists flowing across the road to see the cathedral, but I am happy because I can see them. They are wearing yellow trousers, emerald trousers, blue boots. They are wearing red heels, they are wearing turquoise flats. Having a limited amount of space in their airline suitcases, they have thought for a long time about what they would like to wear to see this place. They have thought about what the place would like to see them wearing, and what their fellow tourists would like to see them wearing and what I, sitting in this cafe, would like to see. And even if they discovered—as soon as they got here—that their clothes were wrong for the weather, the setting, the occasion, they're stuck with them and they're going to stick with them. The tourists are mostly women, or perhaps I don't notice the men, who wear shapeless beige pants, shapeless beige hats. The younger women are all dressed the same, in the current fashion. The older women are dressed either more primly or more provocatively than the younger women, but always in reaction to them.

The locals flow past the cafe and over the river in a stream of grey.

I came to this cafe because it is not the cafe across the street. This is not the cafe I would normally come to. The cafe across the street is better but there are advantages. From this cafe I can see the beautiful people in the cafe across the street: sitting at that cafe, I could only be amongst them. As I sit at this cafe I develop a certain affection for the people here, which makes me feel I might have chosen this cafe after all. They are not so well dressed as the people in the cafe across the street, and more of them smoke. Their voices are more raucous, and especially their laughter. Their hair is not so expensive and is stiffer and comes in colours that are easily named.

I resemble neither the people in this cafe nor the people in the cafe across the street.

Despite being worse than the cafe across the street, this is not a cheap cafe, but I am getting good value. What am I paying for? The view of the cathedral (which is not so good from the better cafe)? If the tourists block the view, should I pay less? Do the tourists worsen the view? I don't think so. They make me sure the view is a view, even though sometimes they are in the way of it.

A few hours ago I was on a plane. I have time to kill, too much time in the wrong place. The day has stretched and I have baggy hours that should be taken in, taken up. There is nothing to do with this time but put some alcohol into it. Alcohol alters time like tourists alter space: it becomes more colourful, more transient, more purposeful, sillier.

The tables in this cafe are close, very close. A man sits down at the table next to me. I wonder whether he is French, whether he is foreign, whether he is a tourist. I also wonder whether I could say hello to him, in French or in English; whether we would like each other, whether we could sleep together. Two days ago I was upside down in a tall hotel that reached toward the sky: 37th floor. My spine's compressed after the flight, my legs unwisely crossed. I have never felt like this before. It feels old.

The man, who is older than me and not particularly attractive, orders some food in English. On the plane I ate things I had never eaten before, things I didn't particularly want to eat at times I didn't want to eat them. The more of the things I ate, the more I accepted them, and the more angry I became in the times between, when they did not appear.

I order. *Madame*, says the waiter, *Mademoiselle* (more of the Madame nowadays). I am careful to speak French with an English accent. It would be disrespectful to the waiter, to the foreign man at the next table, to show too much proficiency.

The man's order arrives quickly. It is a steak. Portions in this cafe are large: portions on the plane were small, but still I feel full. I can smell his steak. It is the steak I did not order, both for financial reasons and because I thought it might be too filling. He eats his steak quickly with no wine. I eat a croque monsieur slowly with a glass of wine which is not the cheapest on the menu. I drink so the scum of things rises to the surface, so I can begin to write about them. I spent my money on wine: he spent his money on steak.

Who got the best value? He takes a bottle of Coca-Cola out of his bag and, when the waiter goes away, takes surreptitious sips. Perhaps he is economising too.

The man with the steak looks at my legs which gives me permission to look at the message he is typing into his mobile phone. I cannot see it as the glass reflects. I feel cheated.

I am tired and slightly drunk and still hungry. He is full of steak and Coca Cola and, presumably, energy: enough energy to cross the road and walk up the steps inside the tower of the cathedral, which I have never entered.

In a few hours I will travel back to the airport to take another plane. Sitting here I am already waiting to wait. I have had so many last times here, it is impossible to tell whether this will really be the last. Time, when it is limited, is more beautiful. My wine tastes of smoke, incense. How can I leave this place? How can I stop watching the flow of tourists across the road? (Look! That one dropped something. It catches the light, shines! A valuable or just a cellophane wrapper? She does not notice, does not return to pick it up.) I drink my wine. I eat my bread, put Paris into my mouth endlessly. Look! Look at the bread, the wine, the tourists! I can't stop looking at them.

The man at the next table takes a large, black camera from his bag and photographs what remains of his steak with a lens so long he can he barely fit it between himself and his plate. The camera makes a soft expensive click. As soon as I hear this I know I could never talk to him. He finishes quickly, and quickly asks for 'the check'. He gets up from his table and leaves.

He has hidden the remaining part of his large steak under his napkin. Our tables are close, so close I can still smell the steak, so close I could reach across and take it, eat it.

Blue

I AM ON HOLIDAY IN A HOUSE WITH NO MIRRORS.

My friend is here with me. She has agreed to share the house I have rented for the summer.

I see my friend in her swimsuit. She has good legs, very good legs. I can see them but I cannot see my own legs. If I want to see my own legs I must stand on the chair in the dark dining room and look at them reflected in the glass of the dark picture above the mantelpiece. Even attached to no one I know they are my legs and I know they are not so good as my friend's.

The house is furnished with the dirt-ring of its owners' lives. Some of it is very good, some of it is very bad, but nothing is perfect. The chairs' legs are curved and polished, but they are chipped. The curved handles of the teacups are chipped, but they have gold rims, which are worn. The bathroom cabinet is made of chipboard. Its legs are missing. It has only plastic and metal stumps.

The decor of the house is blue, which I do not like. My friend is reading a book I do not like. Though I have not read it, I know it is not a good book. This makes things more even.

The bottom of the swimming pool outside the house is painted blue. The sky is blue, unclouded. The grass is blue in the strong sun. I pull a long string of skin, like dried grass, from a scratch on my shin. My friend jumps into the pool, her good legs flow behind her like contrails.

I read my book.

Fin de Collection

A FRIEND TOLD ME TO BUY A RED DRESS IN PARIS BECAUSE I AM leaving my husband. The right teller can make any tale, the right dresser can make any dress look good. Listen to me carefully: I am not the right teller.

Even to be static in Saint Germain requires money. The white stone hotels charge so much a night just to stay still, just so as not to loose their moorings and roll down their slips into the Seine. So much is displayed in the windows in Saint Germain: so little bought and sold. No transactions are proposed that are not so weighty for buyer and seller as to be life-changing. But, for those who can afford them, they no longer seem to matter.

The women of the quarter are all over 40. They smell of new shoe leather. I walk the streets with them, licking the windows. Are we only funning that we could be what is on display? It is impossible to see what kind of women could inhabit those dresses but some do, some must. Nobody here is wearing them.

Amongst the women I am arrogant. I retain my figure without formal exercise. I retain my position as a wounded woman like something in stone, infinitely moving and just a little silly. In order to retain my position I must be wounded constantly. This is painful, but it is a position I have become used to.

We turn into Le Bon Marché department store, the women and I, *Vogue* heavy in our shoulder bags.

There is nothing like Le Bon Marché if you are rich and beautiful. But if you are not rich or beautiful, it doesn't matter. The store has its own rules. It is divided into departments: fashion, food, home. It is possible to find yourself in the wrong department but nothing bad can happen here and, although you may be able to afford nothing, it costs nothing to look.

Le Bon Marché is always the same and always different, like those postcards where the Eiffel Tower is shown a hundred ways: in the sun, in fog, in sunsets, in snow. It may look different in Spring or Autumn, at Christmas or Easter, but the experience it delivers is always the same.

There are no postcards of the Eiffel Tower in the rain but it does rain in Paris, even in August. And when it rains, you can shelter in Le Bon Marché, running between the two ground-floor sections with one of its large orange paper bags suspended over your head (too short a dash to open an umbrella).

Inside is perpetual summer. Customers complaining of being too hot are forced to take off their coats beneath the stencils of artificial flowers that bloom across midwinter walls. The orange paper carrier bags are not made for real weather, either. Once wet their dye leaks onto hair, coats, and leaves orange stains on pale carpets, clothes, floorboards...

*Fin de collection d'éte.* In Le Bon Marché it is already Autumn. The new collections are in order. They do not privilege experience. With time they will deteriorate, unbalance, as each key piece sells out, leaving a skeleton leaf of basics, black and grey. One can commit too early of course. A key piece bought nearly in style will merely foreshadow the version available when the style is at its height.

In 35 degree heat, we bury our faces in wool and corduroy. We long for frost, we who have waited so long for summer. To change clothes is to take a plunge, to holiday. Who cares if we cannot afford to leave Paris. In the *passerelle*, the walkway between the store's two buildings, a tape-loop breeze, the sound of water, photographs of a beach...

There is something about my face in the mirrors that catch it. Even at a distance it will never be right again, not even to a casual glance. Beauty: it's the upkeep that costs, that's what Balzac said, not the initial investment.

*Je peux vous aider?*

The salesgirl asks the fat woman with angel's wings tattooed across her back. She mouths, *Non*, and walks, with her thin companion, into the *passarelle*, suspended.

# FIN DE COLLECTION

The first effect of abroad is strangeness. It makes me strange to myself. I experience a transfer, a transparency. I do not look like these women. I want to project these women's looks onto mine and with them all the history that has made these women look like themselves and not like me.

From time to time I change my mind and sell my clothes. I sell the striped ones and buy spotted ones. Then I sell the spotted ones and buy plaid. Does it get me any closer? At the checkout, the thin girl in her checked jacket looks more appropriate than me, though her clothes are cheaper. This makes me angry. How did her look slip by me? I was always too young. And now I am too old.

I cannot forgive them. I forgive only the beauties of past eras: the pasty flappers, the pointed New Look-ers. They are no longer beautiful. They cannot harm me now. These two are not even the beautiful people. It's more that they're so much less unbeautiful than everyone else. Please remember, we are in Le Bon Marché. Plunge into the metro if you want to encounter the underground of the norm.

Even your other women seemed tame until I saw them through your eyes, until I saw the attention you paid them. I no longer know the value of anything. And if you do not see me, I am nothing. From the outside I look together. I forget that I am really no worse than anyone else. But how can I go on with nobody, with no reflection? And how, and when, and where can I be inflamed by your glance? I can't be friends with your friends. I can't go to dinner with you, don't even want to.

But why does the fat woman always travel with the thin woman? Why the one less beautiful with one more beautiful? Why do there have to two women, one always better than the other?

*Je peux vous aider?*

*Non.* There are no red dresses in Le Bon Marché. *It isn't the dress: it's the woman in the dress.* (Chanel. Or Yves Saint Laurent.) Parisiennes wear grey, summer and winter: they provide their own colour. I have learned to imitate them. *Elegance is refusal.* (Chanel. Or YSL. Or someone.) To leave empty-handed is a triumph.

In any case come December the first wisps of lace and chiffon will appear and with them bottomless skies reflected blue in mirror swimming pools.

To other people, perhaps, I still look fresh: to people who have not yet seen this dress, these shoes, but to myself, to you, I can never re-present the glamour of a first glance.

To appear for the first time is magnificent.

Joanna Walsh is a writer and illustrator. Her work has been published by, amongst others, *Granta Magazine*, Tate, *The Guardian, 3:AM Magazine, The White Review*, Routledge Porn Studies, Union Books, and the *Journal of the London Institute of 'Pataphysics*. Besides illustrating for publications worldwide, she has created large-scale artworks for the Tate Modern and The Wellcome Institute. Her visual diary site, *Badaude*, was a Webby Awards Honouree in 2008.